WATCH OUT, Little Narwhal!

Jane Riordan

Richard Watson

bookoli

And the unicorn of the sea, it's **Narwhal Ma.**

"Look at me swim," squeaks Narwhal Small.

"I'm the fastest and the finest of them all!"

But this little narwhal doesn't look where he's going.

This little narwhal shows no sign of slowing.

WATCH OUT, little narwhal...

"My silly tusk," says Narwhal Small. "It causes such trouble, it's no use at all."

But a friend **with tentacles** is here to help...

But this little narwhal doesn't look where he's going.

This little narwhal shows no sign of slowing.

WATCH OUT, little narwhal!

CRASH!

Poor little narwhal is

completely stuck.

Wedged
in
the
ice,

what terrible luck.

"My silly tusk," says Narwhal Small.

"It causes such trouble, it's no use at all."

But a **big, strong** friend is here to help...

It's
Polar
Pete!

He stamps on the ice with a **thud** and a **thump**.

CRACK!

Small is free with one final jump.

"Look at me swim," squeaks Narwhal Small. "I'm the fastest and the finest of them all!"

But this little narwhal doesn't look where he's going.

This little narwhal shows no sign of slowing.

WATCH OUT, little narwhal!

"My silly tusk," sighs Narwhal Small.
"It causes such trouble, it's no use at all."

But a long, shiny friend is here to help...

It's Simi Seal!

She uses her snout to nuzzle in the sand,

Soon Small is free, just as Simi had planned.

The next day Small and his Ma and Pa,
are invited to a party
that's not too far.
They arrive at the place,
what a sight meets their eyes!

A party just for Small,
what a surprise!

All the tiny creatures are waiting side by side,
then one asks, very shyly, if they can have a ride.

WHEEEEE!

"Look at us go," squeaks Narwhal Small.

"My tusk is useful after all!"

"I may be different, I may look strange,

but it's special being different, and I wouldn't want to change.

I love being just the way I am."

And with a flick of his tusk, away Small swam.